First published 2005 by Walker Books Ltd
87 Vauxhall Walk, London SE11 5HJ

10 9 8 7 6 5 4 3 2 1

Text and illustrations © 2005 Susanna Gretz

This book has been typeset in Little Dracula

Printed in Singapore

British Library Cataloguing in Publication Data: a catalogue record
for this book is available from the British Library

ISBN 1-84428-002-0

www.walkerbooks.co.uk

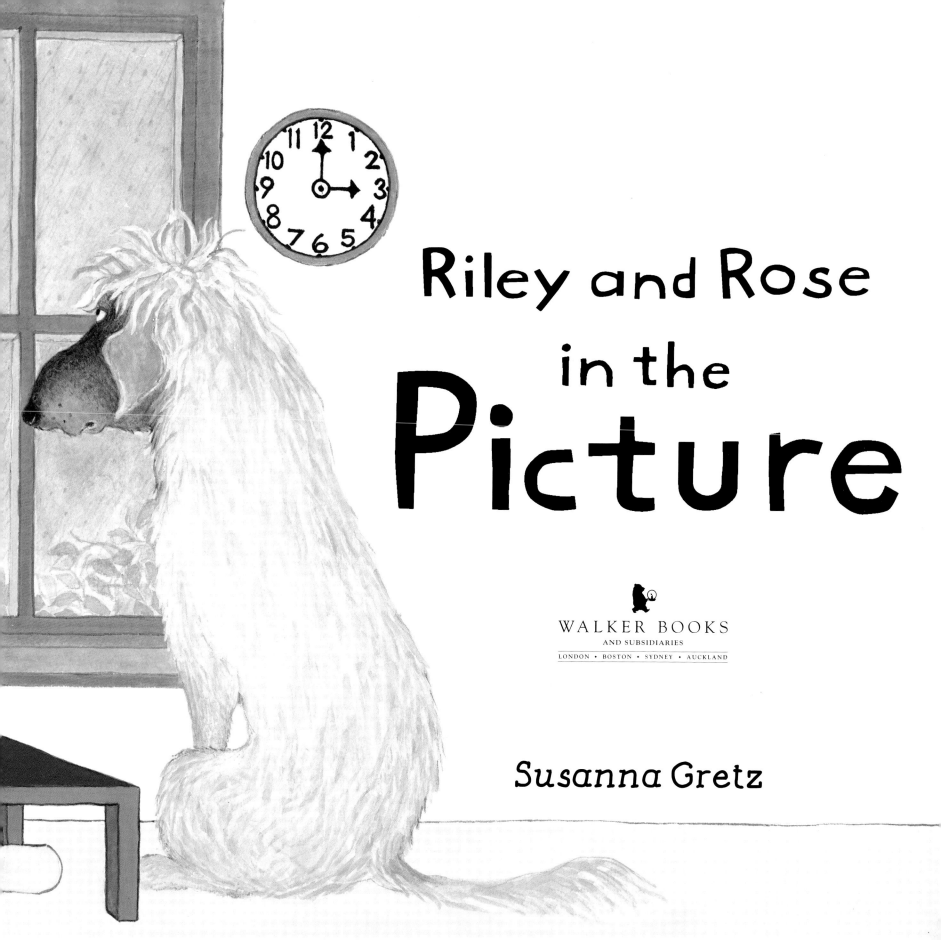

Riley and Rose
in the
Picture

WALKER BOOKS
AND SUBSIDIARIES
LONDON · BOSTON · SYDNEY · AUCKLAND

Susanna Gretz

It's raining hard.
"Let's stay indoors
 and draw pictures,"
 says Riley, the dog.
"But we mustn't fight,"
 says Rose, the cat.
"Of course not," says Riley.
"Let's draw trees and bugs
 and carrot cake," says Rose.
"No way," says Riley,
"I'm going to draw dots
 and lines and shapes."

Riley draws lots of dots.

"Those are raindrops," says Rose.

"No," says Riley. "They're dots."

"No," says Rose.
"They're raindrops and
 this is a great big tree."
"That's not a tree," says Riley.
"That's a mess."

"It's a tree in the rain," says Rose.
"**MESS**," says Riley.
"But let's not fight."

"Now I'm going to draw circles," says Riley.

"Those are bugs," says Rose.

"No," says Riley. "They're circles."

"They're **BUGS**," says Rose, "with legs and spots."

Rose draws lots of bugs.
Then she changes one bug into the sun
and some other bugs into flowers.
She adds some grassy lines too.

Riley doesn't like Rose's garden.

"Watch me draw a spiral," he says.

Rose draws a spiral too, but she adds a stick.

"Now it's a lollipop," she says ...

and she plants some spirally lollipops in her garden.

"Which kind do you want, Riley?" she asks.

"There's orange, lemon, raspberry ripple…"

"Don't be ridiculous," says Riley, "those aren't **REAL** lollipops."

"They are," says Rose, "but let's not fight."

Now Riley sticks up a long sheet of paper.

He draws a straight line all the way across it ...

and a zigzag line on top.

"Those are tents," says Rose.

"No," says Riley. "They're triangles."

"No, tents," says Rose.

She adds some flags.

"Those are little triangles," says Riley.

"No," says Rose. "They're flags. And it's dark out, and I'm in my cosy tent!"

She draws a long yellow tail peeking out from her tent.

"You're spoiling my triangles," says Riley.

"I'm not," says Rose.

And they fight about it.

"How about one more shape?" says Riley.

He draws a square. Rose tries to draw one too.

"That's not a square," says Riley. "It's a rectangle."

"No," says Rose, "it's a boat with big zigzag waves!"

"Don't be ridic—" but Riley stops.

The truth is, he loves boats.

"All aboard, Riley!" says Rose.

Riley looks at Rose's boat.

He gives it a big red triangular sail.

"There's a storm coming!" says Riley.

"With zigzag lightning!" says Rose.

They hop aboard.

"Wow!" says Riley.

"Cat overboard!" yells Rose.

"Dog to the rescue!" calls Riley.

He tosses Rose an old bench ...

and they paddle back to shore.

"Let's dry off," says Riley.

They both have a good shake.

The rain has stopped, the sun's come out,
and it's time for some cake....

"With sprinkles on top," says Rose.

"They're just like dots," says Riley.

"Well, OK," says Rose, "dots.
But shall we eat it all up?"

"You bet!" says Riley.

So they did.